S.S.F. Public Library
West Orange
840 West Orange Ave.
South San Francisco, CA 94080

P9-EGL-995

SEP 2016

1 CD

LOUKOUMI's GOOD DEEDS

Nick Katsoris

Illustrated by Rajesh Nagulakonda

Loukoumi's Good Deeds

CD Narrated by:

Jennifer Aniston & John Aniston

Featuring the Voices of:

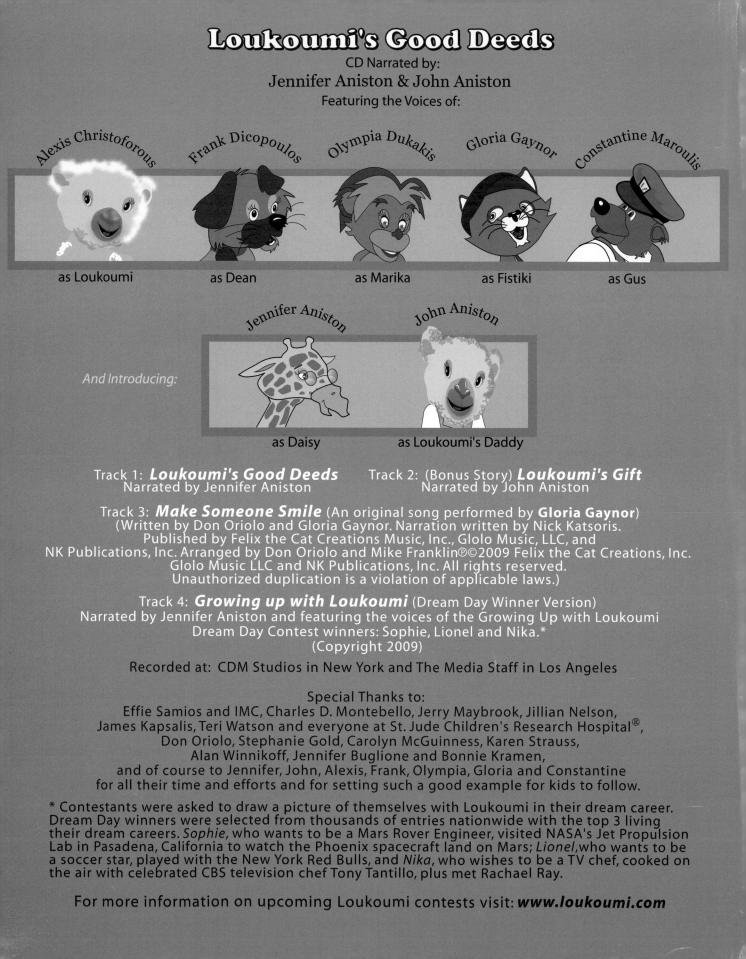

Alexis Christoforous — as Loukoumi

Frank Dicopoulos — as Dean

Olympia Dukakis — as Marika

Gloria Gaynor — as Fistiki

Constantine Maroulis — as Gus

And Introducing:

Jennifer Aniston — as Daisy

John Aniston — as Loukoumi's Daddy

Track 1: *Loukoumi's Good Deeds*
Narrated by Jennifer Aniston

Track 2: (Bonus Story) *Loukoumi's Gift*
Narrated by John Aniston

Track 3: *Make Someone Smile* (An original song performed by **Gloria Gaynor**)
(Written by Don Oriolo and Gloria Gaynor. Narration written by Nick Katsoris.
Published by Felix the Cat Creations Music, Inc., Glolo Music, LLC, and
NK Publications, Inc. Arranged by Don Oriolo and Mike Franklin®©2009 Felix the Cat Creations, Inc.
Glolo Music LLC and NK Publications, Inc. All rights reserved.
Unauthorized duplication is a violation of applicable laws.)

Track 4: *Growing up with Loukoumi* (Dream Day Winner Version)
Narrated by Jennifer Aniston and featuring the voices of the Growing Up with Loukoumi
Dream Day Contest winners: Sophie, Lionel and Nika.*
(Copyright 2009)

Recorded at: CDM Studios in New York and The Media Staff in Los Angeles

Special Thanks to:
Effie Samios and IMC, Charles D. Montebello, Jerry Maybrook, Jillian Nelson,
James Kapsalis, Teri Watson and everyone at St. Jude Children's Research Hospital®,
Don Oriolo, Stephanie Gold, Carolyn McGuinness, Karen Strauss,
Alan Winnikoff, Jennifer Buglione and Bonnie Kramen,
and of course to Jennifer, John, Alexis, Frank, Olympia, Gloria and Constantine
for all their time and efforts and for setting such a good example for kids to follow.

* Contestants were asked to draw a picture of themselves with Loukoumi in their dream career.
Dream Day winners were selected from thousands of entries nationwide with the top 3 living
their dream careers. *Sophie*, who wants to be a Mars Rover Engineer, visited NASA's Jet Propulsion
Lab in Pasadena, California to watch the Phoenix spacecraft land on Mars; *Lionel*, who wants to be
a soccer star, played with the New York Red Bulls, and *Nika*, who wishes to be a TV chef, cooked on
the air with celebrated CBS television chef Tony Tantillo, plus met Rachael Ray.

For more information on upcoming Loukoumi contests visit: ***www.loukoumi.com***

Dedication

To Daisy and the Judge for always doing something nice!

To Jennifer, John, Alexis, Frank, Olympia, Gloria and
Constantine for doing something nice for kids!
To my parents for setting a "nice" example,
and always to Voula, Dean and Julia.

Copyright © 2009, **Nick Katsoris**
Dream Day Press/NK Publications/ Loukoumi Books
Loukoumi is a registered trademark.
All rights reserved.

No part of this book or CD may be reproduced, stored in a retrieval system, or transmitted by any means,
electronic, mechanical, photocopying, recording, or otherwise, without written permission from the author.

Illustrations by **Rajesh Nagulakonda**

$2 from the sale of each book will benefit St. Jude Children's Research Hospital ®
St. Jude Children's Research Hospital® is one of the world's premier pediatric cancer research centers.
Its mission is to find cures for children with cancer and other catastrophic diseases
through research and treatment. For more information, please visit **www.stjude.org.**

St. Jude Children's
Research Hospital
ALSAC · Danny Thomas, Founder
Finding cures. Saving children.

It was the first day of school.
Loukoumi was riding the bus, when all of a sudden
it came to a complete stop.
Loukoumi saw crossing guard Gus helping
an elderly giraffe across the street.

Loukoumi called out to Gus and said,
"That was very nice of you!"

And Gus replied, "Helping others is a wonderful thing!

Make someone smile
Do a good deed
Lend a hand to a friend in need

Whatever you do
Whatever you say
Do something nice for someone today!"

Loukoumi then realized all the nice things
she could do for all the special people in her life.

She could help her mother
clean her room,

she could help her daddy wash the car,

or she could call her grandma and grandpa lamb
and tell them that she loved them.

Later that day Loukoumi saw her friend
Fistiki standing by a tall tree in the school yard.
A red balloon was caught in the tree and
beneath it was a kitten crying.

Fistiki jumped up into the tree and
rescued the red balloon for his new friend.

"Do you know that kitty?" asked Loukoumi.

"I don't," replied Fistiki, "but that doesn't
mean you shouldn't help her.
Helping people is fun!

Make someone smile
Do a good deed
Lend a hand to a friend in need

Whatever you do
Whatever you say
Do something nice for someone today!"

Loukoumi then followed Fistiki to their classroom.

Their teacher, Miss Effie, handed out
colored paper and crayons and asked
the class to draw a picture for someone they love.

Loukoumi's friend Dean drew a card
for his grandpa's birthday.

Loukoumi saw the card and said,
"That was very nice of you."

And Dean replied:

"I didn't have enough money in my piggy bank
to buy him a gift, so I wanted to make something
nice for my grandpa's birthday.

Make someone smile
Do a good deed
Lend a hand to a friend in need

Whatever you do
Whatever you say
Do something nice for someone today!"

After school, Loukoumi and her friends went to the park to play soccer.

Loukoumi jumped up in the air with all her might
and made a great kick, but then fell down
and scraped her knee.

Her friend Marika ran over to Loukoumi
with a band-aid and placed it on Loukoumi's knee.

"Thank you Marika. I feel much better now,"
Loukoumi said.

"Helping you feel better,
makes me feel better," Marika said.

"Make someone smile
Do a good deed
Lend a hand to a friend in need

Whatever you do
Whatever you say
Do something nice for someone today!"

After she left the park, Loukoumi went home

and cleaned up her room,

helped her daddy wash the car,

and called her grandparents
and told them that she loved them.

That night, Loukoumi's parents tucked her
into bed and her Daddy said, "Thank you Loukoumi
for all the nice things you did today."

Loukoumi leaned over and kissed
her Mommy and her Daddy and then said:

"It makes me happy to make someone smile
To do a good deed
To lend a hand to a friend in need

Whatever I do
Whatever I say
I am glad that I did something nice today!"

THE END

ABOUT THE AUTHOR

Loukoumi's Good Deeds is Nick Katsoris' third book in the series following *Loukoumi* and the iParenting Media Award winning *Growing Up With Loukoumi*, both of which have been translated into Greek by Livanis Publishing. In 2008, Katsoris sponsored the *Growing Up With Loukoumi* Dream Day contest based on the book's theme that kids can be anything when they grow up if they believe in themselves. After 200 storytime events nationwide and thousands of entries, 3 kids were selected to live their Dream Days. One visited NASA to witness the Phoenix spacecraft land on Mars, another played soccer with the New York Red Bulls, and a third cooked on the air with CBS chef Tony Tantillo, plus got the chance to meet Rachael Ray.

Nick is a practicing attorney as General Counsel of the Red Apple Group in New York and President and Founder of the Hellenic Times Scholarship Fund, which has awarded over 500 scholarships. He lives in Eastchester, NY with his wife Voula, a real estate attorney, and their children Dean and Julia.

- *"Charming...Beautiful...Gives confidence."* **Martha Stewart**
- *"Loukoumi is Darling!"* **New York Daily News**
- *"Adorable!"* **Good Day New York,** Fox-TV
- *"Powerful!"* **NBC-TV**
- *"Inspiring!"* **The Morning Show** with Mike & Juliet
- *"Big stars, and teaches kids a lot!"* **WCBS-TV**

- **iParenting Media Award Winner**

Book Includes Narrated CD Featuring:

Oscar Winner OLYMPIA DUKAKIS • Grammy Winner GLORIA GAYNOR
CBS News Anchor ALEXIS CHRISTOFOROUS • *Guiding Light's* FRANK DICOPOULOS
American Idol's **CONSTANTINE MAROULIS** & Gloria Gaynor's original song *Believe*
$2 from the sale of each book benefits a national children's charity

English Edition   **Greek Edition**   **Loukoumi Plush**   **Loukoumi T-Shirt**   **Greek Edition**

WWW.LOUKOUMI.COM